Copyright © 2005 by Kim Xiong
Heryin Books
1033 E. Main St., #202, Alhambra, CA 91801
Printed in Taiwan  All rights reserved.
www.heryin.com

Library of Congress Cataloging-in-Publication Data
Xiong, Kim, 1975-
The little stone lion / written & illustrated by Kim Xiong.
-- 1st English ed.  p. cm.
Summary: A little stone lion, smaller than a cat,
tells about the Chinese village that it guards.
[1. Statues--Fiction. 2. Lions--Fiction. 3. China--Fiction.]
I. Title.  PZ7.X53Lit 2005    [E]--dc22    2005013001
ISBN 0-9762056-1-0

# THE LITTLE STONE LION

KIM XIONG

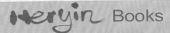 Books

Alhambra, California

I am the guardian spirit
of the village.

I am the village's only stone lion,

Its only
guardian
spirit.

Although I'm smaller than a cat,

I'm older than even the
oldest village elder.

Everyone loves me.
When New Year comes,
they don't forget me.

Children walking at night
look at me and feel safe.

Old people caress my head and sigh, thinking back to when they were children.

I remember everything.
I remember all the people
and all that has happened.

Children grow up and

leave the village...

Maybe they will forget me...

But I will remember
them and miss them.

I won't forget anyone.

I am the village's stone lion,

The village's only guardian spirit.